EINSTEIN

THE CLASS HAMSTER

SAVES THE LIBRARY

EINS

THE CLASS HAMSTER

Janet Tashjian

EINSTEIN

SAVES THE LIBRARY

Illustrated by
Jake Tashjian

Christy Ottaviano Books

HENRY HOLT AND COMPANY ~ NEW YORK

Henry Holt and Company, LLC
Publishers since 1866
175 Fifth Avenue
New York, New York 10010
mackids.com

Henry Holt® is a registered trademark of Henry Holt and Company, LLC.
Text copyright © 2015 by Janet Tashjian
Illustrations copyright © 2015 by Jake Tashjian
All rights reserved.

Library of Congress Cataloging-in-Publication Data
Tashjian, Janet.
Einstein the class hamster saves the library / Janet Tashjian ; illustrated by Jake
Tashjian.—First edition.
    pages   cm
Summary: When Principal Decker closes Boerring Elementary School's library due
to severe budget cuts, Einstein and his friends in Ms. Moreno's class
try to reopen it by planning fund-raisers, including shooting a video
that stars Einstein and Marlon the turtle.
ISBN 978-1-62779-061-1 (hardback)
[1. Hamsters—Fiction. 2. Schools—Fiction. 3. Humorous stories.] I. Title.
PZ7.T211135Ejm 2015   [Fic]—dc23   2014045668

Henry Holt books may be purchased for business or promotional use.
For information on bulk purchases, please contact the Macmillan Corporate
and Premium Sales Department at (800) 221-7945 x5442 or by e-mail
at specialmarkets@macmillan.com.

First Edition—2015
Printed in the United States of America by R. R. Donnelley & Sons Company,
Harrisonburg, Virginia

1 3 5 7 9 10 8 6 4 2

TO OUR FAVORITE PEOPLE
IN THE WORLD—
LIBRARIANS

ALSO BY JANET AND JAKE TASHJIAN

The Einstein the Class Hamster Series:
Einstein the Class Hamster
Einstein the Class Hamster and the Very Real Game Show

The My Life Series:
My Life as a Book
My Life as a Stuntboy
My Life as a Cartoonist
My Life as a Joke
My Life as a Gamer

"The most precious things in life are not those you get for money."

—ALBERT EINSTEIN

"I know money can't bring happiness— but sometimes money is what you need!"

—EINSTEIN THE CLASS HAMSTER

CHAPTER ONE

A CRISIS

"**W**elcome to another episode of

ANSWER THAT QUESTION!

Today our contestant is Bonnie Thompson!"

Einstein pointed to Bonnie, quietly writing at her desk.

"I'm not sure she knows she's on your show today," Marlon said.

"Maybe if I command her to hear me, she'll come over." Einstein closed his eyes and concentrated on getting Bonnie to stand up. *You want to be on my game show. You can't wait to hear the latest Tasty Tidbit.*

But Bonnie continued to work.

"That went well," Marlon said.

Einstein persisted. "She's getting up! She's coming over!

I HAVE MAGIC POWERS!

"She's sharpening her pencil," Marlon said.

Einstein ignored him. "The topic of today's first round is CLOUDS. I hope all you contestants brought your umbrellas!"

Einstein watched sadly as Bonnie sharpened her pencil and returned to her seat.

"Looks like it's raining on **YOU**," Marlon said.

Show business had its ups and downs—didn't Marlon know that? And as far as "up" was concerned, nothing made Einstein happier than seeing his friend Ned, who was the only one of his classmates who could actually hear him.

"I just overheard Principal Decker talking to Ms. Moreno," Ned said. "I'm not sure what they were talking about, but it sounded like bad news."

Einstein threw himself into the pile of shredded paper in the corner of his tank. First Bonnie, now this?

Ms. Moreno addressed the class. "Everyone in their seats. I have an announcement to make."

Einstein buried himself deeper in his paper cave.

"Psssst!" Marlon called from his tank. "Maybe the bad news is that they're getting rid of Twinkles— maybe it's actually GOOD news."

Twinkles the Python was the scourge of Boerring Elementary. He was Principal Decker's favorite, but he spent every waking minute trying to eat the other class pets.

Einstein scurried out from his hiding place to hear what Ms. Moreno had to say.

"Our school's in a financial crisis," she said. "And Principal Decker has to make some serious budget cuts."

Einstein crossed his fingers and toes. *Please say you're getting rid of Twinkles!*

"As of today," Ms. Moreno continued, "our school library will be closed."

"**NOOOOOOOO!**" Einstein shouted.

Closing the library? Einstein couldn't imagine anything worse.

9

EINSTEIN'S TASTY TIDBITS

Rain, snow, sleet, and hail are all forms of precipitation that fall from clouds. Clouds are formed by tiny drops of water, sometimes millions of pounds of them. The main types of clouds are cumulus (puffy, like cotton), cirrus (wispy and thin, high in the sky), and stratus (flat, like layered sheets).

SHOULD I?

Fog is a kind of stratus cloud, appearing very low to the ground.

CHAPTER TWO

A WORD ABOUT LIBRARIES

Einstein jumped onto his hamster wheel and started to run.

HOW COULD THEY CLOSE THE LIBRARY?

It was the HEART of the school!

He ran faster and faster as images filled his head:

- Following his parents through the tunnels of the school until he came to a room full of books—like a thousand Christmases rolled into one.
- Lying on the rug, spending hours enjoying the illustrations in a favorite picture book.
- Burying his head inside the latest volume, inhaling that new-book smell.

Einstein had to see if this horrible news was true. He snuck out of his tank and down the hall. He scurried into the hole in the wall behind the water fountain and entered the complex system of tunnels his ancestors had dug years before. After several minutes, he arrived in the reference section of the library (his favorite part).

Ms. Remington, the librarian, was packing up her desk with Principal Decker.

It IS true, Einstein thought. *Ms. Remington—please don't go!*

Principal Decker looked almost as depressed as Ms. Remington did.

"We're going to reopen this library as soon as possible," the principal said. "It's my highest priority."

DO THESE BOOKS MAKE ME LOOK FAT?

BOX O' BOOKS

Ms. Remington carefully wrapped the photographs of her students at Storytime. *Everyone looks so happy in those pictures*, Einstein thought. *Everyone loves stories.*

"My hands are tied," Principal Decker continued. "I wish there was something I could do."

As Einstein looked at how beautiful Ms. Remington had made the library over the years, he thought he might cry. The construction-paper flowers, the beanbag chairs, the books in colorful bins all neatly labeled—Ms. Remington had put so much effort into this school.

Principal Decker led Ms. Remington

to the library door, then took out a large padlock. "There's a whole procedure we have to follow when a library closes," he told her. "Hopefully we can reopen soon."

From his hiding place, Einstein watched the principal padlock the door. He couldn't remember ever feeling so sad.

EINSTEIN'S TASTY TIDBITS

The oldest federal cultural institution in the United States is the Library of Congress. It was established by President John Adams in 1800. It's the largest library in the world, with 838 miles of bookshelves.

Americans visit libraries three times more often than they go to the movies!

CHAPTER THREE

WE NEED A PLAN

When the rest of the class went to recess, Ned tried to calm Einstein down. "Get off that wheel—you'll waste away to nothing."

But Einstein continued to run. "We've **GOT** to save the library!" he panted.

"I'm sure if we put

our heads together, we can come up with something," Ned said.

"Ahh, here comes the traitor now." Einstein gestured to Principal Decker, who was wearing Twinkles like a scarf.

"With your precious books gone, maybe you'll have time for some other activities," Twinkles hissed. "Like playing hide-and-**SQUEAK**—I mean **SEEK**—with your friends."

"Go away," Einstein said. "You're making things worse."

"Are you sure you don't need a hug?" Twinkles continued. "It might cheer you up."

"Get lost," Marlon said. "No one wants to be squeezed and eaten today, thank you very much."

Ned ducked behind the shelf
and gestured for the class pets to
be quiet.

"I don't want to close the library
either, but money doesn't grow on
trees," Principal Decker told Ms.
Moreno.

Einstein rolled his eyes. "Thanks for the botany lesson, Principal Decker."

"You know what they say," Ms. Moreno added. "'A room without books is like a body without a soul.'"

"That's a quote from Cicero," Einstein whispered to Marlon.

Ms. Moreno smiled. "The library is the soul of our school, Principal Decker. We need to find a solution."

"Ms. Moreno, we're behind you one hundred percent," Einstein shouted.

Ned waited until the others left before coming out from his hiding place. "We're going to do this," he told Einstein. "We're going to save the library."

Einstein wanted to believe him.

After recess, all the students wanted to talk about were ways to save the library.

"We can have a bake sale," Bonnie told Ms. Moreno. "You can make your famous turducken cupcakes."

Ms. Moreno beamed. "My cupcakes ARE delicious. But I'm afraid this is going to take more than a bake sale."

"How about a skateboarding competition?" Ricky asked. "We can race around town and take donations."

"We can have a carnival in the parking lot," Ned suggested. "With a Ferris wheel, games, and cotton candy!"

Ms. Moreno added all the suggestions to the board. Inside his tank, Einstein made his own list.

"How about if we chain ourselves to the radiators?"

"This school doesn't have radiators," Marlon said.

"Or go on a starvation diet?"

"You wouldn't last a day without food."

"Why don't we go to tonight's town meeting," Ned suggested, "and tell everyone why they can't close the library."

"That's an excellent idea," Ms. Moreno said. "Why, I bet—" But before she could finish her sentence, Ms. Moreno was fast asleep on her feet.

Ned tiptoed back to his seat, not wanting to wake her up.

Ms. Moreno's students were used to her frequent napping. Their teacher had the bad habit of staying up all night to watch infomercials, with the disastrous consequence of falling asleep several times during the day. But she was so happy and knowledgeable when awake that her students always covered for her with Principal Decker (who was usually too busy with Twinkles to notice).

"What do you say?" Ned whispered to his classmates. "Should we try and get the Town Board to change their minds?"

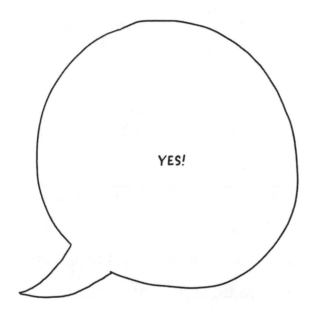

"Yes!" the others whispered back.

Einstein knew his classmates would need lots of research to back up their arguments. Luckily for them, he was a research whiz.

EINSTEIN'S TASTY TIDBITS

Cotton candy has only two ingredients: colored sugar and air. It was originally called "Fairy Floss" and introduced to the masses at the 1904 World's Fair, which also popularized hot dogs, hamburgers, Dr Pepper, waffle cones, and iced tea. Unlike those treats, cotton candy is made of more than 50 percent air. The sugary sweet was invented by a candy maker— and a dentist!

CHAPTER FOUR

WHEN ONLY A LIBRARY WILL DO

Nothing made Einstein happier than doing research. Finding new facts was what he lived for, and now he had a chance to really help his class. He looked up statistics for hours; he scoured town records; he even studied the archive of dusty manuscripts Ms. Remington kept locked away with the town's historical documents.

In looking for information to save the library, Einstein came across lots of GREAT facts that he was excited to use on **ANSWER...THAT... QUESTION**.

He couldn't believe all the new Tasty Tidbits he found:

● The boardwalk in Atlantic City,

New Jersey, is the longest and oldest boardwalk in the world.

- A ten-gallon hat does NOT hold ten gallons. (It doesn't even hold one.)
- An adult dragonfly lives only a few months.
- A giraffe's tongue is so long it can clean its own ears with it.
- One type of hummingbird weighs less than a penny.

There was no doubt about it. Even if he couldn't use any of these Tasty Tidbits to help Ned, learning all these facts made today one of Einstein's **BEST DAYS EVER**.

EINSTEIN'S TASTY TIDBITS

The streets in the game Monopoly were named after real streets in Atlantic City, New Jersey. More than 275 million Monopoly games have been sold, and over 1 billion people have played since the game was invented in 1935. The longest Monopoly game on record lasted for seventy days straight.

CHAPTER FIVE

YOUR RESEARCH ASSISTANT IS READY

Einstein couldn't wait to show Ned all his hard work, but as soon as he saw his best friend's face, he knew something was wrong.

"They refused to let us speak at the town meeting," Ned said. "We need to come up with a Plan B."

"But you're a citizen!" Einstein complained. "They can't stop you from talking at the meeting."

"Apparently they can." Ned pointed to his notebook. "I had lots of good information too."

Einstein was proud of Ned; he'd gotten so much better at doing research since they'd become friends.

"You should start a petition," Einstein suggested. "Get signatures from people who want to keep the library open."

Bonnie skidded over to Ned. "We can make a video and post it on the school's website. What do you think?"

As much as Einstein loved the thought of a petition, dreams of

LIGHTS . . .

CAMERA . . .

ACTION

filled his head.

"I like it," Ned agreed.

"Ms. Moreno does too." Bonnie motioned to Ms. Moreno, now asleep at her desk again. "At least she did a few minutes ago."

"Who should be in the video?" Ned asked.

ME, ME, ME, thought Einstein.

"Ricky said it might be fun to use Twinkles," Bonnie suggested.

NO, NO, NO, thought Einstein.

"He could slither around the library—it might be cool and menacing." Bonnie made some

spooky Halloween
noises.

"Filming Twinkles
is a TERRIBLE
idea," Einstein said.
"It has nothing to do
with saving the library."

"Be quiet," Ned said.

"Are you talking to me?"
Bonnie asked.

"No!" Ned answered.

"But you just told me to be quiet."
Bonnie did NOT look happy.

"He was talking to me!" Einstein
said. "It's not always about you,
Bonnie."

Ned shot Einstein a look to put a lid
on it.

"I think making a video is a GREAT
idea," Ned said. "Let's see what the
others say."

Ned and Bonnie ran out to the school yard to find their friends. Einstein looked down at the stacks and stacks of notes he'd made for Ned.

"They'll use that information someday," Marlon said. "You did a lot of good work."

Einstein didn't tell Marlon about the color-coded map of the school he'd slaved over for hours.

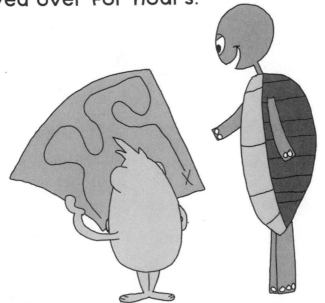

"You don't think they'll make a video with Twinkles, do you? They should shoot a video of us playing **ANSWER...THAT...QUESTION** instead."

"It might be hard since Ned's the only one who can hear us."

Marlon did have a point.

EINSTEIN'S TASTY TIDBITS

The study and art of mapmaking is called CARTOGRAPHY. Because a map is graphic, it's a universal way to convey facts and figures. You can find out lots of information about history by studying maps of a given time period.

Some of the oldest known maps were made in Babylon in 2300 B.C. on clay tablets, but now most people use computers to read them. More than a billion people have downloaded Google

Earth; scientists in England used it to locate a virgin rain forest in Mount Mabu, Mozambique, that was only known locally. The forest is now referred to as "Google Forest."

EVER GET THE FEELING YOU'RE BEING WATCHED?

CHAPTER SIX

MEANWHILE,

AT MS. MORENO'S HOUSE

Ms. Moreno stayed up late watching infomercials and making lots of phone calls to various shopping networks. She wanted to get the best deals on the latest gadgets, and nothing could stop her—not even sleep.

But what kept her awake tonight was trying to come up with ways to save Boerring Elementary's library. She knew the town was in a financial

crisis, but a school **NEEDED** a library.

As she tried to hatch a plan, she ran several carrots and apples through her new juicer. She soaked her feet in a massage tub, tied her hair in a French braid with a fancy clip, exercised along with her EXTREME CARDIO DVD, riveted rhinestones onto the new vest she quilted, applied a cucumber facial mask, ground some fresh peanut butter, and sharpened all her knives and scissors. By early morning, she didn't know how she'd save the library; she just knew she was tired.

"I'm determined to raise the money," Ms. Moreno said to herself. "It might be difficult but—wait, is that a new purse organizer? For just $19.99?" She jumped off the couch and ran to the phone. "What a bargain!"

EINSTEIN'S TASTY TIDBITS

Scientist and inventor George Washington Carver was born into slavery in Missouri in the 1860s. When slavery was abolished, he went to school, eventually getting his high school, college, and master's degrees. He taught agriculture for forty-seven years at Tuskegee University in Alabama, an all-black college.

He encouraged farmers to grow peanuts as an alternative to cotton after the boll weevil destroyed most of the

South's cotton crops. He developed more than three hundred uses for peanuts (which are legumes, not nuts). Believe it or not, two American presidents were peanut farmers: Thomas Jefferson and Jimmy Carter.

I THINK I HAVE A PEANUT ALLERGY. . . .

CHAPTER SEVEN
BONNIE
STEPS IN

"**O**kay, here's the plan." Bonnie was standing next to Ms. Moreno, sound asleep at her desk. "What kind of videos always go viral?"

"Funny animal videos," Ricky answered.

"**EXACTLY**," Bonnie said. "Let's use the class pets."

Einstein put down his pencil. Did he just hear Bonnie right? "Marlon—they're going to make us stars!"

Marlon tucked his head farther inside his shell. "Not everybody wants to be a star. Some of us just want to be left alone."

But Einstein was already getting ready for his close-up. He quickly groomed his fur and filed his teeth. Even if they couldn't hear him on the video, at least he'd *look* great.

Einstein usually was not a hamster who stared at the clock, but today was different. He counted down each minute until school was over and he could finally take his place in front of the camera. When he wasn't watching the clock, he was daydreaming about movie stars and red carpets and

Oscars and interviews and *Access Hollywood* (the hamster version). This was going to be amazing!

"Einstein!" Marlon called. "You're wanted on the set."

Sure enough, Ned, Bonnie, and Ricky were placing a video camera on a tripod next to Ms. Moreno's desk.

It was time to make a movie!

EINSTEIN'S TASTY TIDBITS

During his lifetime, Thomas Edison held patents for more than a thousand inventions, but one of his most famous was the motion picture projector. Other people also worked on creating machines that filmed moving images; Edison called his the Kinetoscope.

The first motion picture ever copyrighted showed Fred Ott—one of Edison's employees—pretending to sneeze. Edison built a movie studio not in

Hollywood, but in New Jersey. His studio made *The Great Train Robbery* in 1903; it was one of the first Westerns and one of the first blockbusters in the silent-movie industry. It cost only $150 to make.

CHAPTER EIGHT
A STAR IS BORN

Einstein knew Bonnie liked to sew and do craft projects, but he hadn't realized she was such a competent director too.

"Okay, let's get Marlon out here," Bonnie said. "A turtle is a great main character."

Marlon??? Einstein thought. *What about me? Hamsters are a hundred times cuter than turtles!*

"We can say, 'Don't stick your head in the sand—libraries are important,'" Ricky said.

"Turtles don't bury their heads in the sand!" Einstein screamed. "You're talking about ostriches—and even **THEY** don't do that!"

He was happy when Ned intervened.

"How about Einstein?" Ned suggested. "People love videos with hamsters and squirrels."

Ugh, don't lump me in with them, Einstein thought. *Squirrels are such HAMS. They never met a camera they didn't like.*

"Let's try Marlon first," Bonnie said. "I've got a good feeling about him." She scooped up Marlon from his lagoon and placed him on Ms. Moreno's desk.

"This isn't fair!" Einstein said. "He doesn't even want to be in your dumb movie! He HATES videos—unlike me, who watches them all the time!"

While the others filmed a few test shots, Ned snuck over to Einstein.

"Calm down. You're making a scene."

"You're the only one who can hear me," Einstein complained.

"Yes, and it's distracting." Ned gave his friend a smile. "You'll get a chance later, I promise."

"Marlon's going to need a thousand takes," Einstein said. "He's not a professional like I am."

Ned tried not to laugh as he headed

to the front of the room. He loved
Einstein, but his friend
could be such a
baby sometimes.

Einstein
scampered out
of his tank to get
a closer look. Was
Ms. Moreno feeding Marlon a snack?

"She's giving him green beans!"
Einstein yelled to Ned. "This is **SO
UNFAIR**."

Einstein scurried along the
bookshelf to see what else he was
missing.

"Marlon, you look hungry," Ms.
Moreno said. "How about some
carrots too?"

"NO, NO, NO!" Einstein shouted. "He doesn't want any more snacks!"

"Yes, I do," Marlon called.

Einstein slumped behind a stack of books. Why was Marlon getting all the attention?

"Hey, look!" Ricky said. "Marlon's chasing an olive across the desk!"

"Olives have pits! Marlon could choke," Einstein cried. "Besides, turtles are too slow to chase things."

Bonnie zoomed in with the camera. The kids all laughed as Marlon chased the olive across the desk.

"Sure, it's cute," Einstein called to Ned. "But how's that going to save the library?"

Ned was too busy praising Marlon to answer.

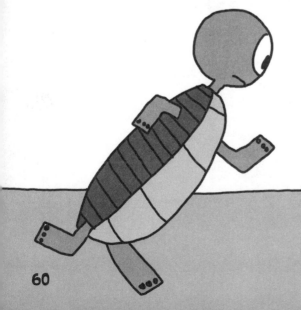

EINSTEIN'S TASTY TIDBITS

Ostriches can go a long time without drinking water; they get water from the plants they eat. Ostriches are so strong that one kick to a lion can be fatal.

An ostrich's brain is smaller than its eyeball, which is the size of a billiard ball. They are the largest, heaviest birds and unable to fly. Ostriches are fast, though, outrunning most of their predators at forty miles per hour. Contrary to popular belief, they do NOT bury their heads in the sand. The myth probably got started because ostriches dig large holes for their eggs and bend down often to turn them. Because an ostrich's head is so small, from a distance it might appear as if it's burying its head.

SO MUCH FOR BEING KING OF THE JUNGLE!

CHAPTER NINE

EINSTEIN'S TURN

"**H**ow about if we do a backup video with Einstein?" Ned suggested.

"A **BACKUP VIDEO**?!" Einstein shouted. "Like I'm some kind of understudy for Marlon?" The situation was completely unacceptable.

"That's a great idea," Bonnie said. "That way we'll have some options."

"Here's your chance." Ned set the

camera up in front of Einstein's tank. "Break a leg."

"Don't say that!" Didn't Ned know how difficult it was to treat a fracture on a hamster?

"Stop being such a diva," Ned said.

As much as Einstein wanted his performance to shine, he also realized the most important part of today was to remember their goal—saving the library.

"I've got some cherry tomatoes,"
Ricky said. "Let's see if Einstein's as
good at chasing things as Marlon."

That's not going to happen,
Einstein thought. *Let me show you
something better.*

To warm up, Einstein started with
a few impersonations—Elvis Presley
and Marilyn Monroe.

Then he juggled four kibbles in the air, faster and faster—until he realized the clumps he'd taken from the bottom of his cage weren't actually food.

After hurrying to wash his hands, Einstein took out his notes. He looked directly into the camera and talked about how important it was to save the school library.

"It almost looks as if he's reading," Ricky said. "That's weird."

"He's got a lot of skills for a rodent," Ned added.

Bonnie looked at Ned suspiciously. "How do you know so much about Einstein? Are you guys friends now?"

"Yeah, my best friend's a hamster," Ned joked. "We have sleepovers all the time."

Einstein stopped reading. Was Ned telling their classmates they WEREN'T friends?

"Okay, that's enough for today," Bonnie said. "I can't wait to get home and edit this footage."

Ned and Ricky both volunteered to help Bonnie over the weekend.

"You know we really ARE friends," Ned whispered to Einstein later. "It's just hard to explain that I have daily conversations with a hamster."

As difficult as it was to hear, Einstein knew it was true. "I wish I could help you edit the video. You KNOW I'm a whiz with sound effects."

"You're a whiz at a lot of things," Ned said. "I'll see you Monday."

"But who am I going home with
this weekend?" Einstein had been so
busy preparing for the video that he'd
forgotten to check the sign-out
sheet.

"Can somebody help me take
Einstein and Marlon to my car?"
Ms. Moreno asked.

Not Ms. Moreno! Didn't any of his classmates want to hang out with him this weekend? No? Anybody?

Ms. Moreno bent down to Einstein's and Marlon's tanks. "Are you two ready for some **FUN, FUN, FUN**?"

Einstein looked at Marlon.

Marlon looked at Einstein.

"Oh brother, another weekend of infomercials," Marlon said.

Einstein watched as Ned, Bonnie, and Ricky hurried to their lockers. It was going to be a loooooong weekend.

EINSTEIN'S TASTY TIDBITS

Is the tomato a fruit or a vegetable? THAT is the question. From a botanical point of view, a tomato is a fruit because it has seeds. But a tomato has much less sugar than other fruits, so for cooking purposes, it's usually considered a vegetable. Eggplants, green beans, cucumbers, and squashes also have seeds, so botanically they're fruits too—yet are considered and cooked as vegetables.

Tomatoes aren't the only fruit that's hard to categorize. Strawberries are not technically berries at all—but believe it or not, bananas are!

CHAPTER TEN

TOO MUCH TV

Ms. Moreno put on the TV the second she walked in the door. Einstein and Marlon watched her cook dinner—slicing, dicing, chopping, paring, mincing, and shredding a counter full of vegetables with the set of twenty knives she kept in a large stand on the counter.

"Please tell me we're getting some of those veggies," Marlon said.

"I can't remember the last time I had a radish," Einstein added.

"And cut into the shape of a rose." Marlon watched Ms. Moreno carve layers of petals into the radishes. "Maybe these kitchen gadgets aren't such a bad idea after all."

When Ms. Moreno went to answer the doorbell, Einstein snuck out of his tank and stole a few cut carrots to share with Marlon.

"Allison, you're a lifesaver!" Principal Decker said as he entered the living room.

"**NO**!" Einstein shouted.

Principal Decker entered the kitchen and shoved Einstein's tank aside to make room for Twinkles.

"What's HE doing here?" Einstein asked.

Principal Decker told Ms. Moreno that his wife had had an allergy attack and he was taking her to the doctor.

She's probably allergic to snakes, Einstein thought.

"I just couldn't bear the thought of Twinkles being alone." Principal Decker hovered over Twinkles's cage as if he were saying good-bye forever.

Ms. Moreno walked Principal Decker back to his car.

"Why hello, you two." Twinkles slid across his tank toward the other class pets. "Looks like we're having a sleepover."

"No one's shutting their eyes now that **YOU'RE** here," Marlon said. "This weekend's officially gone into elevated orange alert."

"Severe red alert," Einstein corrected.

"That's just silly," Twinkles hissed. "No one's going to get eaten in their sleep— at least not until we've played some party games."

"The last time you tried playing a game with us, we were climbing out of your stomach," Einstein said.

"Jonah and the Whale?" Twinkles asked. "I LOVE that game!"

Ms. Moreno did her little happy dance around the kitchen table. "All my favorite pets are here!

This is going to be great!" She offered each of the animals cucumbers with decorative edges.

Einstein and Marlon enjoyed the treat, but Twinkles pushed his aside. "I'm going to wait until later," he said. "When I can get my hands on something a little more **ALIVE**."

"I think he means us," Marlon whispered.

One by one, Ms. Moreno took the tanks into the living room. After two hours of watching back-to-back infomercials for dozens of products, Einstein felt himself getting sucked into the world of gadgets too.

"Those Day-Glo pens look amazing," he told Marlon.

"Don't get taken in by the bells and whistles," Marlon warned.

Einstein ignored him. "And what about that slushie maker? No mess, no cleanup—we can use it when we have our library-saving celebration."

"I'm beginning to understand why Ms. Moreno is so tired all the time," Marlon said. "It takes a lot of willpower to stop watching these infomercials."

Einstein was so entranced by the exciting products that he didn't notice Twinkles slithering out of the tank and into his.

MR. SLUSHIE!
O MESS! NO CLEANUPS!

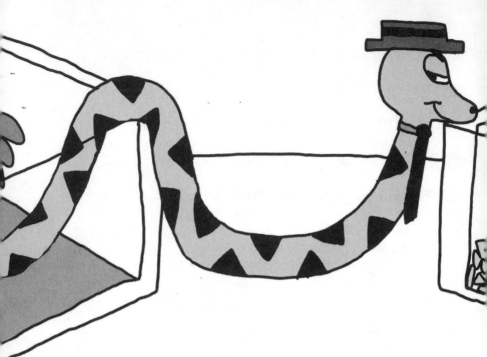

As Einstein searched the tank for a
pencil to write down the 800 number
for the slushie maker, he noticed
Twinkles, just inches away.

"Too bad your little pal Ned isn't
here to save you," Twinkles said.

Einstein cowered in the corner of
the cage, looking for a way out.

"Don't fight it," Twinkles told him. "Just *chillax*."

"I HATE those fake combination words," Einstein said. "Can't you find a REAL word to use?"

"Don't be *redonkulous*," Twinkles chided.

"Stop it!" Einstein screamed as he fought off the python. "Proper language is important!"

"There'll be plenty of time to make up new words when you're inside me." Twinkles wove his way around Einstein several times.

Einstein watched Marlon hurrying out of his lagoon to help. That was the problem with a turtle trying

to save you—it usually got there
too late.

Thankfully Ms. Moreno hurried into
the room. "Twinkles!" she cried. "What
are you doing out of your tank?" Ms.
Moreno carefully unwound the snake
from Einstein.

"Hel-lo, I'm a python," Twinkles said. "You can't give me a cucumber, stick me next to a tasty rodent, and expect me to just sit there. You're a teacher—don't you know how the food chain works?"

"You poor little hamster!" Ms. Moreno told Einstein. "The class would never forgive me if anything happened to you."

Einstein spent the rest of the night cuddled in Ms. Moreno's lap, keeping his eye on Twinkles to make sure he stayed away from Marlon too.

By the time the weekend was over, Ms. Moreno had ordered a twisty-turban, spray-on tanner, a bouncy pillow, and an alarm clock that changed colors. Sadly, not the slushie maker.

Einstein hated to admit it, but he couldn't wait to go back to Ms. Moreno's house to watch more infomercials. Next time without Twinkles.

EINSTEIN'S TASTY TIDBITS

All living things need energy, and a food chain is how energy gets transferred from one species to another. Some living things are PRODUCERS that CREATE energy and some are CONSUMERS that USE energy. Plants are producers; animals are consumers.

If even just one part of the food chain is removed, it can have devastating effects on the other groups.

There are four main types of consumers in a food chain:

1. Carnivores, who eat other animals
2. Omnivores, who eat other animals as well as plants
3. Herbivores, who eat only plants
4. Scavengers, who eat dead animals

CHAPTER ELEVEN

YOU CALL THIS A VIDEO?

Before class started, Einstein told Ned about his exciting time with Ms. Moreno. "You really should think about getting that slushie maker. It was amazing."

"I could've used it this weekend," Ned said. "I worked hard editing that video with Bonnie and Ricky."

Bonnie looked at Ned suspiciously.

"You're talking to yourself again, Ned. Want to watch the video?"

Einstein and Marlon scurried to the edge of their tanks so they could see. Bonnie hit PLAY. Music filled the room.

"I like the opening theme song," Marlon said.

Bonnie told the others she had written the song with her computer's music program. For a moment Einstein felt bad—it would've been fun to be part of the creative team instead of almost being eaten by Twinkles. He'd just have to settle for being the star of the *Save the Library* video.

"Watch this part—it's great." Ned turned up the volume.

Einstein watched Marlon scurrying across the screen, chasing the olive.

"You sped up the film," Marlon said. "It looks like I'm running superfast."

That's a first, Einstein thought. He inched closer to the screen as the camera zoomed in on his tank. "This is where I talk about all the great reference books in the library!" He quieted the others down so he could hear.

But instead of listening to himself talk about his favorite books, the on-screen Einstein was singing in a super-high voice. About candy corn.

"Why do I sound like a Munchkin
from *The Wizard of Oz*?" Einstein
asked. "And why am I singing about
candy?"

Ned laughed. "Bonnie recorded this

hilarious song, then we sped it up and added it to your video."

"It sounds like I inhaled a helium balloon!" Einstein complained. "I was talking about **BOOKS**, not **CANDY**."

"This is so much funnier," Marlon said.

"I thought so too," Ned agreed.

"IT'S NOT FUNNY," Einstein yelled. "IT'S STUPID! No one's going to watch a hamster sing about candy corn!"

"Why not?" Marlon asked. "The *Hamster on a Piano* video is huge."

"Exactly," Ned said. "Bonnie posted your candy corn video on Sunday, and it's already gotten eight hundred views."

"That's great!" Marlon said.

"It's NOT great!" Einstein replied. "I look like a moron obsessed with candy instead of a hamster who knows a lot about math, art, and science."

"I think candy corn is more fun," Marlon said.

"The last frame of the video asks people to donate to our school

library," Bonnie said. "We've raised five hundred dollars so far!"

Even Einstein had to admit that was a good start.

During the day, students who usually didn't visit the class pets (believe it or not, there were a few) came over to hang out with Einstein and Marlon.

"Hey, Einstein!" Tony said. "Do your candy corn dance!"

"I want my candy corn!" Linda said in a fake, high, and totally annoying voice.

"I was talking about things you can find in the library!" Einstein said. "I was talking about skeletons and Picasso and polygons!"

"The only polygon anyone wants to talk about is an orange, yellow, and white triangle you can eat," Marlon said.

This isn't good, Einstein thought. *Not good at all.*

EINSTEIN'S TASTY TIDBITS

The artist Pablo Picasso produced more than fifty thousand paintings, ceramics, drawings, prints, tapestries, rugs, and sculptures. His full name is actually twenty-three words long: Pablo Diego José Francisco de Paula Juan Nepomuceno María de los Remedios Cipriano de la Santísima Trinidad Martyr Patricio Clito Ruíz y Picasso. No other artist has had more paintings stolen than

Picasso. He created his first painting when he was nine years old, and the first word he ever spoke as a child was the Spanish word for *pencil*.

CHAPTER TWELVE

A GIANT
MISTAKE

For the next week, the entire school got into the act—bringing in bags of candy corn and making candy corn puppets, candy corn banners, candy corn dioramas, and candy corn posters. The students took turns singing the candy corn song over the PA system each morning.

Reading the comments on YouTube didn't help either. On the one hand,

Einstein enjoyed being called "cuddly," "adorable," and "lovable," but he DIDN'T like being referred to as "silly," "nutty," and "hare-brained." (That one really hurt—hares have terrible long-term memories. A hare would never be able to remember all the Tasty Tidbits Einstein used in his show.)

"I feel like a moron," Einstein said. "The butt of a lame joke."

"A joke that's raised seven hundred dollars to save the library so far," Ned said. "Stop complaining."

Einstein didn't have to be a math genius to know that the town needed to raise a lot more money than that to reopen the library.

"I took your suggestion and

started a petition to let students talk at the town meeting." Ned held up a clipboard so Einstein could see all the signatures. "The board said I got enough to speak tonight."

Ned had come such a long way from a few months ago when he was the quietest kid in class with Einstein as his only friend. Now he had enough confidence to ask several hundred people to help his cause.

"Great job," Einstein said. "Let me get my notes to help you prepare."

"Your facts will be really helpful," Ned said. "Unfortunately, I won't be able to tell everyone where I got all this good information."

"That's okay." Einstein had all the faith in the world that Ned would get the job done.

AMANDA TAWKTOO
HUGH JEERS
EILEEN DOVER
WILL U. REED
SEYMOUR BOOKS
JUSTIN TIME
CANDY CRUSH
ROBIN BANKS

But as soon as Einstein saw Ned the next morning, he knew something was wrong. "Didn't they let you talk?" Einstein asked.

"They let me talk, all right," Ned said. "I did a presentation with charts—I even used my father's laser pointer. It was a really professional presentation."

"So what happened?"

"All anyone wanted to do was talk about the candy corn video," Ned said.

"I told you that video was a disaster," Einstein said.

"Looks like Plans A and B both failed."

All the students appeared as if they'd caught the same strain of depression virus—Bonnie looked ready

to cry and Ricky just stared at the
top of his desk in a daze.

"We can't give up!" Einstein said.
"Remember the famous quote: 'It's
not that I'm so smart, it's just that I
stay with problems longer.'"

"Who said that?" Ned asked.

"My namesake, Albert Einstein."
Einstein pulled himself up a few
inches taller. "If **HE** didn't give up,
then **WE'RE** not giving up either."

"Hey, do you guys want to come
home with me this weekend?" Ned
asked Einstein and Marlon.

"I can't," Einstein said.

Ned looked at his friend with suspicion. "Why? What's going on?"

"Nothing!" Einstein lied. "I left some things at Ms. Moreno's house."

"He wants to watch infomercials," Marlon said.

Einstein shot Marlon the evil eye. "Blabbermouth!"

"TV addict," Marlon whispered back.

"Just for that, you don't get to use the slushie maker when I finally get it," Einstein said.

"Okay, Marlon, let's go." Ned picked up Marlon's tank and headed home for the weekend.

As Einstein watched them go, he wondered if he was doing the right thing. Shouldn't he be with Ned and Marlon, brainstorming new ways to save the library?

"Looks like it's you and me,

Einstein," Ms. Moreno said as she packed up her things.

That purse organizer really does work, Einstein thought. *What a great purchase.* He happily went home with their teacher for the weekend.

EINSTEIN'S TASTY TIDBITS

It took Albert Einstein a long time to learn to speak. He may have been slow with words, but that's because Einstein thought in pictures. Most of his breakthroughs were not performed in a lab but in his head. He called them *Gedankenexperiments,* which means "thought experiments" in German. For one of his theories of relativity, he imagined how someone traveling on a train would watch lightning bolts hitting the train differently from how someone standing on the platform would see them. His theories might involve a lot of math and physics, but he thought them up first in images. Einstein was *TIME* magazine's PERSON OF THE CENTURY in December 1999—not bad for a daydreamer who hated haircuts and socks.

CHAPTER THIRTEEN
AHA!

Einstein's new strategy was to pretend he was sick so Ms. Moreno would take him out of the tank to sit with her on the couch. And it worked! Once Einstein was settled next to her, he focused on one thing: gaining control of the remote.

When Ms. Moreno left the room to get a cup of tea or a few of the Girl Scout cookies she kept stashed in the cupboard, Einstein changed the channel to a shopping network HE wanted to watch. Enough with the fuzzy clown slippers—what about that musical Twister game? Or the mini-muffin oven? At one point during the evening, Ms. Moreno tried

to put Einstein back in his tank, but Einstein pretended to cry until she let him stay.

Einstein was mesmerized by the cookie-decorating machine, the steam press, the pretzel factory, the jelly bean bank, and the calligraphy kit. His favorite was the automatic coin counter—what a great way to keep track of all the donations his class was receiving to save the library. But thinking about the padlocked library suddenly made him feel bad.

The shopping network host

interrupted Einstein's reverie. "And here's something for all you book lovers out there: beautiful bookplates!"

Both Einstein and Ms. Moreno sat up straight.

"Handsome, personalized bookplates for your home library!"

THIS BOOK
BELONGS TO . . .
YOU!

The announcer continued. "With gold-embossed lettering."

"Gold," Ms. Moreno said in a trance.

"Embossed," Einstein added.

They both stared at the television as the host browsed through a large room filled with shelves and shelves of books.

Looking at all those wonderful books, Einstein couldn't get the Albert Einstein quote out of his head: *It's not that I'm so smart, it's just that I stay with problems longer.* Had he abandoned the library problem in favor of watching TV with Ms. Moreno? Einstein scurried back to his tank and his piles of notes.

He spent the next few hours

reviewing his research until he stumbled onto a piece of information he'd missed before. *This could be it!* Einstein thought. *A way to save the library!* He'd need Ned's help, of course. Maybe some others' too.

As he congratulated himself on a job well done, Einstein had no idea that across the room Ms. Moreno was hatching a plan of her own.

EINSTEIN'S TASTY TIDBITS

The oldest form of money was probably cattle, which people traded for goods and services, as far back as 9000 B.C. The first coins, from around 2000 B.C., were shaped like cattle and made out of bronze. America's initial paper money was issued in 1690 in Massachusetts. Before that, people traded deer and elk skins, which is why the word *buck* is used to describe money.

The only woman to appear on any

U.S. paper currency is Martha Washington. Her portrait was on the one-dollar silver certificate in 1886, 1891, and 1896. No other women have been featured on U.S. paper currency since then.

YOU SAID ONE BUCK, RIGHT?

CHAPTER FOURTEEN

TELLING THE OTHERS

Einstein sharpened his pencil to take notes. He loved Mondays!

"I really bonded with Ms. Moreno this weekend," he told Marlon.

"Did you bond over musical waffle irons?"

"For your information, not every infomercial product is musical." Einstein didn't tell Marlon that upon closer inspection, the automatic coin counter did, in fact, play "The Star-Spangled Banner."

"I have a plan I think will work, but I need your help." Einstein handed Ned a piece of paper.

"This is soggy," Ned said.

"It was in my cheek pouch," Einstein answered.

"Your handwriting is terrible," Ned complained.

"JUST READ IT!" Einstein said.

Ned squinted to read Einstein's tiny hamster handwriting. "Hey! This could work!"

Principal Decker strode into the room carrying Twinkles.

"Okay, everyone!" Ms. Moreno said. "Saturday morning we're having a giant yard sale to raise money for the library."

"A SCHOOL yard sale," Marlon joked.

Bonnie's hand shot up. "Can I help?"

"There'll be lots of things for everyone to do," Ms. Moreno said. "I just sent an e-mail to all your parents too."

"Will this mess up your plan?" Ned whispered to Einstein.

"Let's try her plan first," Einstein

said. "We'll keep mine as backup."
Einstein looked at Ms. Moreno handing out assignments to his classmates. As much as he was bothered by her in the past for luring contestants away from **ANSWER...THAT... QUESTION**, he had to admit she really cared about her students.

"Are you sure you want to do this?" Principal Decker asked their teacher. "Even if you raise a lot of money, there's no guarantee it'll be enough to reopen the library."

"We have to try," Ms. Moreno said.

"Okay, Saturday morning it is," Principal Decker agreed.

EINSTEIN'S TASTY TIDBITS

Francis Scott Key was a thirty-five-year-old lawyer who was negotiating with the British to release an American prisoner during the War of 1812. The British agreed to release the prisoner, but only after they attacked Fort McHenry in Baltimore. Francis Scott Key witnessed the bombarding of the fort from the deck of a truce ship; in the morning, he watched the troops at Fort McHenry replace the war-torn U.S. flag with an even larger one.

While on the boat, he wrote a poem that later became "The Star Spangled Banner." It was published in September 1814. When the poem was turned into song, it was set to the tune of a lighthearted British ditty. The song was named the national anthem in 1931. The flag that flew over Fort McHenry that day now rests in the Smithsonian Institution in Washington, D.C.

CHAPTER FIFTEEN

WILL IT WORK?

On Saturday morning, several cars pulled into the school parking lot. Einstein recognized Ned's parents' car, as well as Ricky's and Bonnie's. He was excited to see the school librarian, Ms. Remington, again.

Suddenly an eighteen-wheeler pulled into the parking lot.

"It's showtime!" Ms. Moreno said.

Ms. Moreno, wearing overalls and

I BRAKE FOR LIBRARIES

work gloves, opened the truck's large
door. Inside, the truck was stacked
floor to ceiling with all of Ms.
Moreno's infomercial gadgets. She
stood on the bed of the truck and
addressed parents and students.
"Let's unload this baby!"

Ms. Remington, the parents, and
the students made a human conveyor

belt and unloaded the truck onto the rows and rows of tables Mr. Wright, the custodian, had set up in the parking lot. Soon the tables were full of furry shelves, cat mittens, a french fry holder for your car, and a scale in the shape of a dodo bird. By the time they finished unloading the truck, there was a line wrapped twice around the school with eager shoppers.

HEYWOOD
JAHELPME MOVE

"Ms. Moreno is donating all this to the school?" Ricky asked. "She's single-handedly saving the library."

"Not single-handedly." Bonnie gave Ned and Ricky each a large bag. "We're going to help her."

Ned and Ricky looked inside the bags, then back at Bonnie.

"You can't possibly think—" Ricky said.

"That we're going to **WEAR** these?" Ned finished.

"Ms. Moreno isn't the only one who should make a sacrifice," Bonnie said. "Besides, do you know how long it took me to make these costumes?"

Bonnie dragged the boys inside to change. When they all emerged a few minutes later, Einstein and Marlon burst out laughing.

"Don't say a WORD," Ned said. "I'm embarrassed enough as it is."

Bonnie hooked up her music player to the sound system and hit PLAY. The candy corn song filled the air. Everyone sang along as Bonnie, Ned, and Ricky performed the infamous dance in the candy corn costumes Bonnie had made.

"This is **GREAT**," Einstein said. "Such school spirit."

"As long as YOU aren't the one doing the dance this time," Marlon said.

"Exactly."

"I've never seen Ned and Ricky so embarrassed," Marlon said. "But Bonnie sure seems to be having fun."

Einstein clapped along with the other students as Ms. Moreno continued to sell her gadgets.

Ms. Moreno's plan was working!

EINSTEIN'S TASTY TIDBITS

Dodo birds lived on the island of Mauritius in the Indian Ocean for millions of years, but they became extinct within a century after explorers visited the island in 1598. Dodos were three-foot-tall, flightless birds that weighed fifty pounds. Because humans—and the animals they brought with them—were their first predators, dodos were very trusting and not prepared to defend themselves.

Another extinct flightless bird species WAS prepared to defend itself: the Terror Bird of South America. At ten feet tall, they were one of the toughest carnivores of prehistoric times, grabbing large prey with their pickax beaks and throwing them against the ground to kill them. Luckily for neighborhood pets, Terror Birds are now extinct too.

CHAPTER SIXTEEN
PLAN B

By the end of the day, Ms. Moreno's donations raised several thousand dollars for the Boerring Elementary library. Ms. Remington gathered the students and parents to lead them inside to finally unlock the library doors.

Principal Decker stood on the back of the truck and addressed the crowd. "Boerring Elementary

appreciates everyone's hard work
today, but, unfortunately, there's a
lot of paperwork to reopen a library."
He pulled at his tie as he spoke. "It's
going to take a few weeks before the
library can officially reopen."

"WHAT?" Einstein said. "We can't
wait that long."

Ned and his friends weren't happy

either. "Ms. Moreno donated all this stuff," Ned said. "We worked all day."

"And don't forget the money we raised from the video," Bonnie said.

"Plus, we dressed up like candy corn!" Ricky added.

"I'm sorry," Principal Decker said. "I'll get started on this first thing Monday morning."

No one in the crowd was happy.

"It looks like we need to implement Plan B," Einstein whispered.

"I thought Plan B was making the video," Marlon said.

"Okay, then it's time for Plan C. Or is it Plan D?"

"It's too dangerous," Marlon said.

"Sometimes if you want to succeed, you have to take a risk." Einstein tiptoed out of his tank and approached Twinkles.

"I need you to do something," Einstein told the python.

"Does it involve having a friend for dinner?" Twinkles asked. "Namely you?"

"It's not for me—it's for the school."

When the python heard Einstein's

plan, he looked at the hamster—not in his usual "Can I eat you?" way, but more thoughtfully.

"Count me in," Twinkles said.

"I hope you're not going to regret this," Marlon told Einstein.

"I hope so too," Einstein said as he watched Twinkles coil up next to him. Now all Einstein had to do was talk to Ned.

"Are you sure?" Ned asked after he heard the plan. "This could backfire."

Einstein told Ned there was no other choice if they wanted to open the library today.

"Okay," Ned said. "Here goes." He turned to the crowd of students and parents. "Somebody help! Twinkles is trapped inside the library!"

Principal Decker jumped off the truck and raced between the tables. "How did my Twinky get into the library—it's locked!"

"He looks scared," Ned said. "You've got to get him out!"

Principal Decker threw open the school doors and ran inside. "**I'M COMING, TWINKLES!**"

"Did Twinkles get in through the window?" Bonnie pressed her face against the library door. Inside, Twinkles was slithering across the shelves.

It DID seem like a mystery—unless you knew about Einstein's secret tunnel.

"I hope this wasn't a giant mistake," Marlon said.

Einstein agreed.

Principal Decker continued to yank on the padlocked door. **"TWINKLES!"**

"Come on, Twinkles," Einstein said. "Let's see those acting chops."

"Don't mention 'Twinkles' and 'chops' in the same sentence," Marlon said.

Einstein watched as Twinkles pretended to be lost and afraid. It was the best python performance he'd seen since watching old horror movies at Ned's house.

Ms. Moreno faced down the principal as he yanked on the padlocked doors. "You might have to unlock these doors to save Twinkles."

Principal Decker skidded down the hall to his office. He rummaged through his desk until he found the key.

"PAPA'S COMING, TWINKLES! **PAPA'S COMING!**" Principal Decker cried.

Principal Decker was so nervous, Ms. Remington had to take the key from him to unlock the door. He ran inside and scooped Twinkles into his arms.

"You owe me one," Twinkles whispered to Einstein when he came out. "And I know just how you can pay me back."

But Einstein needed to focus on the rest of his plan. As soon as Principal Decker was about to lock the door again, he nudged Ned forward.

Ned unfolded the piece of paper Einstein had given him earlier. "Once a town library is reopened," Ned read. "It must remain open."

Principal Decker grabbed the paper from Ned's hand. "Where did you find this?"

"With the town's historical documents," Ned answered. "The rule was written almost a hundred years ago."

Ned went to the historical research section and pulled open the book Einstein had told him about.

Ms. Moreno walked to the front of the crowd carrying several sacks of money. "And after today's sale, I think we **CAN** leave the library open."

Principal Decker looked around the room. He might have unlocked the door to save Twinkles, but he was keeping it unlocked for his students. "The library is officially reopened!" he shouted.

Einstein had to give credit where

credit was due. "We couldn't have done this without you," he told Twinkles.

"I know how you can pay me back," Twinkles repeated.

"If it involves digestion, I'm not interested."

"Now that I know how to get into your secret tunnel," Twinkles said, "perhaps I can pay you a surprise visit sometime. We can hang out."

"I warned you," Marlon said. "You'll never be safe from Twinkles again."

As everyone celebrated, Ms. Moreno asked Ned where he'd found out about such an obscure town ruling.

Ned looked over at Einstein and smiled. "Where you find everything—

IN THE LIBRARY."

EINSTEIN'S TASTY TIDBITS

Several of the body's organs are used in the digestive process: To digest even a piece of fruit, the mouth, esophagus, stomach, small and large intestines, gallbladder, pancreas, and liver are all involved.

The first step in the digestive process is CHEWING. The average body makes between one and three pints of saliva each day to break down food. The muscles in the esophagus contract in waves to move food down, so even if you are standing on your head, food will make it into your stomach.

CHAPTER SEVENTEEN

THE LIBRARY REOPENS

Monday morning, students and teachers gathered in the hall outside the library. Ned had Einstein tucked inside his jacket pocket.

"I don't want to miss anything!" Einstein said. "Cut to the front of the line!"

Ned told Einstein to settle down.

The other teachers were so impressed by Ms. Moreno's sacrifice,

they spent the weekend doing some
shopping of their own. The library
was now filled with upholstered
chairs, woven rugs, and well-placed
lamps. And books! Rows and rows
and rows of new books for all the
students to enjoy. Books about

anatomy and Native Americans and crafts and music and art, and novels and chapter books and picture books. There were more books than Einstein had ever seen.

Even though she'd parted with a lot of her possessions, no one in the room was happier than Ms. Moreno, fast asleep on the new, comfy window seat.

"She really is a hero," Ned said.

"So are you," Einstein added.

As if she knew someone was talking about her, Ms. Moreno woke with a start. She stretched and yawned, then called Ned over.

"You seem quite fond of Einstein," Ms. Moreno said.

You don't know the half of it, Ned thought. He could feel Einstein moving around in his pocket.

"It may sound funny, but I swear that hamster inspired me to sell all that stuff I didn't need."

"It doesn't sound funny at all," Ned answered.

Ms. Moreno looked around the room at the students reading and enjoying books. "I DO miss my rhinestone coffeemaker," she said. "But there's an additional purchase I couldn't resist."

She pulled a book from the shelf and opened it. Affixed to the inside front cover was the most beautiful bookplate Ned had ever seen. It read: EX LIBRIS—BOERRING ELEMENTARY.

"Ex libris is Latin and means 'from the library of.'" Ms. Moreno ran her finger along the embossed lettering. "It's a way of saying that these books belong to our school and that no one can take them away."

Einstein poked his head out from Ned's pocket. The bookplates from the infomercial! Embossed! In Latin! And gold!

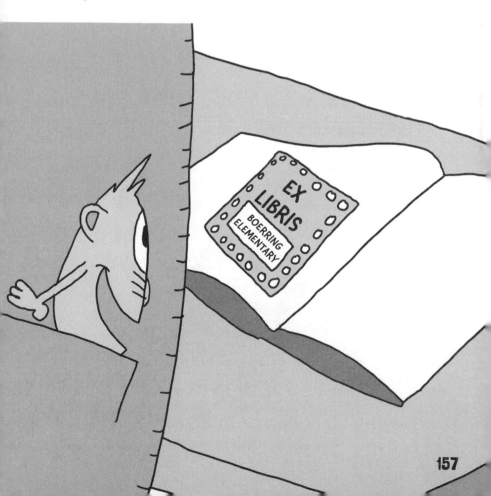

EX LIBRIS

BOERRING ELEMENTARY

Bonnie spied another box behind Ms. Moreno. When she asked about it, Ms. Moreno smiled sheepishly. "Okay, I made TWO additional purchases." She reached behind her and pulled out the box.

Einstein's face lit up. "**THE SLUSHIE MAKER!**"

"I thought we could enjoy some slushies while we read," Ms. Moreno said.

"As long as they're not turducken slushies," Ned whispered to Bonnie.

Ms. Moreno clapped her hands and called her students over to the window seat. "Who wants to hear a story?" she asked.

It was the greatest question in the world—a question no one could ever say no to. Einstein settled in with his classmates as Ms. Moreno began to read.

ONCE UPON A TIME . . .

ANSWER... THAT... QUESTION!

⚡LIGHTNING ROUND⚡

Let's see how well you remember your facts!

1. What is the largest library in the world?

2. What are the puffy types of clouds called?

3. A giraffe's tongue is so long it can clean its own ears—true or false?

4. Some living things in a food chain are producers—the others are called what?

5. What was the original name for cotton candy?

6. Ostriches bury their heads in the sand— true or false?

7. What was probably used as the oldest form of money?

8. George Washington Carver discovered 300 uses for which legume?

9. The streets in the game Monopoly are named after streets in what city?

10. What caused dodo birds to become extinct?

11. Albert Einstein thought in pictures— true or false?

12. A ten-gallon hat holds ten gallons of water—true or false?

13. An omnivore eats only plants—true or false?

14. What is the study of maps called?

15. What is the first step in the digestive process?

16. The first movie Thomas Edison made was of a man pretending to do what?

17. Who wrote the lyrics to "The Star-Spangled Banner"?

18. Which two U.S. presidents were peanut farmers?

19. The virgin rain forest discovered with Google Earth is now called what?

20. What was Pablo Picasso's first word?

How did you do?

1. *THE LIBRARY OF CONGRESS*

2. *CUMULUS CLOUDS*

3. *TRUE*

4. *CONSUMERS*

5. *FAIRY FLOSS*

6. *FALSE*

7. *CATTLE*

8. *THE PEANUT*

9. *ATLANTIC CITY*

10. *HUMANS*

11. *TRUE*

12. *FALSE*

13. *FALSE*

14. *CARTOGRAPHY*

15. *CHEWING*

16. *SNEEZE*

17. *FRANCIS SCOTT KEY*

18. *THOMAS JEFFERSON AND JIMMY CARTER*

19. *GOOGLE FOREST*

20. *PENCIL*

SPECIAL FEATURES

BLOOPERS AND DELETED SCENES

167

FIND OUT MORE

Want to find out more information about my Tasty Tidbits? Explore your local library or check out these online sites:

CLOUDS:
sciencekids.co.nz/sciencefacts/weather/clouds.html

LIBRARIES:
loc.gov/about/fascinating-facts
against-the-grain.com/2011/06/five-fun-facts-you-may-not-know-about-libraries

COTTON CANDY:
yurtopic.com/food/cooking/cotton-candy-facts.html

TASTY TIDBITS ON PAGES 30-31:
tealdragon.net/humor/facts/facts.htm

MONOPOLY:
hasbro.com/monopoly/en_US/discover/about.cfm

CARTOGRAPHY:
academic.emporia.edu/aberjame/map/h_map/h_map.htm

PEANUTS:
nationalpeanutboard.org/classroom-funfacts.php
nationalpeanutboard.org/classroom-carver.php

THOMAS EDISON:
inventors.about.com/library/inventors/bledison.htm

OSTRICHES:
funshun.com/amazing-facts/ostrich-birds-facts.html
kids.nationalgeographic.com/kids/stories/animalsnature/animal-myths-busted

TOMATOES:
healthdiaries.com/eatthis/15-fun-facts-about-tomatoes.html

FOOD CHAIN:
kidskonnect.com/subjectindex/15-educational/science/77-food-chain.html

PABLO PICASSO:
pablopicasso.org/picasso-facts.jsp

ALBERT EINSTEIN:
alberteinsteinsite.com/einsteinfunfacts.html

CURRENCY:
factmonster.com/ipka/A0774850.html

"THE STAR-SPANGLED BANNER":
songfacts.com/detail.php?id=2102

FLIGHTLESS BIRDS:
dodobird.net

DIGESTION:
sites.google.com/site/digestivesystem3051/fun-facts-2

About the Creators of the
EINSTEIN THE
CLASS HAMSTER
series

Mike Morelli

JANET TASHJIAN has written many books for elementary, middle grade, and young adult readers. She loves doing school visits around the country, talking to students about reading, cartoons, and how important it is to have chocolate around when you're writing. Her son, **JAKE TASHJIAN**, has illustrated eight books for kids, including the award-winning My Life series. The Einstein series is based on a comic strip he created in sixth grade. Jake is an avid surfer; Janet is an avid coffee drinker. They live in Los Angeles.

Also by

JANET TASHJIAN

with illustrations by

JAKE TASHJIAN

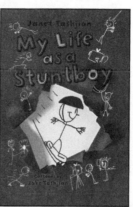